MAROONED WITH DARCY

A Sensual Pride & Prejudice Variation

Abbey North

BLURB

Lizzy and Jane are on a ship bound for America to stay with Mr. Collins's younger brother when they meet Mr. Bingley and Mr. Darcy. Mr. Darcy's disapproval of the burgeoning affection between Jane and Charles is painfully obvious, and Lizzy does her best to thwart his attempts to stop the developing relationship. She is puzzled by how invigorating it can be to trade barbs with Darcy, and he seems to enjoy it as well, but he is the last man she could ever soften toward due to his haughty manner and prideful ways.

When their ship wrecks, Lizzy and Darcy end up stranded alone on an island. As the days pass while they await rescue, the undeniable attraction between them becomes overwhelming, leading them both to act. Even as Lizzy succumbs to the temptation and falls for Darcy, she wonders if he is indeed the last man she would ever marry, or if she has been fooling herself about the strength of her emotions all along?

While Abbey sometimes writes sweet JAFF, this is strictly SENSUAL.

The timeline is different here. Mr. Bennet died shortly after Mr.

Collins came to Longbourn and left after Lizzy's rejection. Darcy and Charles never came to Netherfield. Darcy and Lizzy are meeting for the first time aboard the ship bound for America.

CHAPTER ONE

Lizzy smiled when Jane laughed, a warm and engaging sound she'd heard far too infrequently from her eldest sister in the last two years, since Papa passed away and life became a struggle. That it was the charming Mr. Charles Bingley who elicited the laugh further pleased her. She couldn't think of a better match for her sister, and it had surely been providence that they were all traveling on the same boat from London to Boston, bringing her uncomplicated sister into the same sphere as the congenial and equally unfussy Mr. Bingley.

Without her permission, her gaze darted briefly to Mr. Bingley's companion, the stern and grim-faced Mr. Darcy, who made no attempt to hide his disapproval of Jane and Mr. Bingley's interaction. It was unfortunate providence had also seen fit to ensure he trailed along behind his friend as they embarked on a great adventure at Mr. Bingley's insistence.

Darcy had made no attempt to hide his dismay at the journey Mr. Bingley wanted to undertake, seeing no reason to tour the Colonies. That was just one of his many strongly held opinions of which Lizzy had heard over the last two weeks as they sailed together.

With a sigh, trying to dismiss the tiresome man from her thoughts, she returned her gaze to Jane and Mr. Bingley again. The two sat an appropriate distance apart, but there was warmth in their interactions, and she couldn't help thinking they had a future between them, unless Mr. Darcy managed to tarnish it.

She finished her dinner, keeping a complacent eye on her sister and a more watchful one on Mr. Darcy, who continued to scowl in the other couple's direction. She shook her head, wondering how he could stand to be so stern and disapproving of someone he'd barely met, though of course, it was hardly surprising.

The Bennet girls were in reduced circumstances. Though they had once been a landed gentleman's daughters, they now lived in a small house on Longbourn land, provided through the sheer generosity of Mr. Collins, and Lizzy suspected only at her dear friend Charlotte's behest, who had the misfortune of being married to Mr. Collins.

She shuddered, briefly remembering the time Mr. Collins had come to Longbourn when her father still owned it, hoping to acquire a wife from among one of the five Bennet sisters. Mercifully for Jane, she had spent the summer recovering from a nasty bout of cholera, so she'd been frail, spending most of her time in bed. That had allowed her to elude the distasteful eye of the reverend.

Unfortunately for Lizzy, his eye fell on her instead, and though her mother had encouraged the match, Mr. Bennet had endorsed her robust rejection. Perhaps Lizzy would've changed her mind if she'd realized that just months later, her life would alter irrevocably, but her father had seemed hale and strong at the time, and it was a distant fear that someday he would pass away before them with none of the daughters married.

No, she couldn't imagine she could've been happy as Mr. Collins's wife. Her friend Charlotte had stepped in, acquiring Mr. Collins's attention after Lizzy's harsh rejection, and she wished her friend well. Charlotte seemed content enough in the match, and she was mistress of Longbourn now. They were still good friends, and Charlotte didn't lord it over her in any fashion that she was only staying on their land in the small house due to her benevolence.

Mr. Collins was a different matter, and she winced when she thought about him again. He lost no opportunity to be smug about the position of power he held over them, or to remind them they lived at his largess. She could only hope she and Jane were making the right decision by accepting Mr. Collins's younger brother's invitation to come visit him in Boston.

They were hoping to make fine

matches, or at least find some prospect that would alleviate the concern Mrs. Bennet displayed for their future. More pragmatically, it would help with their aunts and uncles' burdens, since meeting their financial obligations fell to the Gardiners and the Philipses at this point.

Perhaps Lizzy would be the only one searching for a beau or a promising position when she reached Boston though. She eyed Jane and Charles speculatively as they finished the meal.

"Would you fancy a turn about the deck, Miss Jane? I find it good for one's digestion." Mr. Bingley issued the invitation with a wide grin.

"Perhaps you would do better with some reflection in your cabin," said Mr. Darcy, apparently trying to dampen Mr. Bingley's enthusiasm.

Lizzy gritted her teeth and glared at him before smiling at Mr. Bingley. "I am certain Jane would much appreciate the idea, as would I. There is nothing quite as invigorating as a walk." It was certainly different aboard a ship though. Gone were the days of meandering through Longbourn Park and occasionally finding herself on Netherfield Park land as well.

Netherfield had been

abandoned for years, and though the skeletal staff did their best to maintain its former glory, it was a losing battle. Lizzy really liked the wildness that had settled over it, along with the unexpected delight of wandering through meadows to find a field of lilacs, or growths of wildflowers that had never been allowed to flourish in the days of Lord Horn, who had been the previous owner before his death, when he had kept landscaping staff.

That was certainly a contrast to Longbourn, which had always been neat and tidy, except for a few wild areas. Now, it seemed almost barren, since Mr. Collins was the frugal sort. He'd done away with all unnecessary expenditures, including planting flowers that were suitable only for decoration. They had a leaner existence at Longbourn, and Lizzy had always tried to accept that rather than resent how he'd changed things in her father's stead.

She grasped the shawl and wrapped it around her as they walked up the ladder to reach the deck. Though it carried some cargo, the *Corsica* was primarily a passenger ship, so it had most of the modern conveniences and accommodations, but the deck could still be slippery. She took a step forward and almost fell, startled when Mr. Darcy was the one who reached out to keep her from doing so.

He held her for a moment longer than necessary, likely ensuring she was steady, before she nodded her thanks and took a step back. She was more cautious this time when she walked, and she was strangely aware of him hovering nearby as they followed Jane and Mr. Bingley for a turn around the deck.

She deliberately dawdled behind them a little bit, allowing the couple some privacy, and also hoping to speak to Mr. Darcy alone. When sufficient space remained between them, she slowed to a stop and turned to face him. "I wish to discuss something with you, Mr. Darcy."

He scowled. "I can well imagine what it is. You are hoping I will withdraw any objection to Charles and Miss Jane Bennet. I assure you now, that shall not happen, Miss Bennet."

She put her hands on her hips as she glared up at him. "Why ever not? What objection could you have to Jane? She is the sweetest, kindest soul I know."

He arched a brow. "Perhaps she is. I have seen no indication that she is not the most congenial and pleasant sort, but nor have I seen any indication she has true regard for Charles."

Lizzy's mouth dropped open. "Are you blind, sir? Have you not seen how she lights up in his presence, and tonight, she laughed so delightfully? It has been a long time since I have seen my sister with such a carefree manner. I daresay, she prefers Mr. Bingley's company above all others, myself included." She pulled a wry face for a moment, forgetting with whom she was conversing.

His frown only deepened. "Then I submit the likelihood of her troubles being eased might be what encourages laughter, not true affection."

She glared at him as she took a step closer. "How dare you, Mr. Darcy? You do not know my sister, so how can you presume to know her heart?"

He maintained a passive expression, seeming to have no response to her anger. "I heard the rather charming tale of how your mother tried to marry you off to Mr. Collins, and another time, she attempted to steer your sister Mary toward the new vicar in your village, going so far as to try to arrange for them to be compromised alone before you interceded."

Lizzy winced with shame. "That might be true." She cleared her throat. "In fact, it was true. Unfortunately, Reverend Bowers had been a comforting presence to my mother upon Papa's passing, and she thought it was a sound match. She was overzealous in her grief, and I stepped in to prevent any compromise from occurring." She shrugged. "Jane is not my mother, nor am I. If she has an interest in Mr. Bingley, it is because she likes him as a person, not as a possible purse. You have underestimated her, sir."

He snorted. "I see little evidence of that."

"Perhaps you should open your eyes and look harder, Mr. Darcy. You have allowed your own prejudice to sway your actions and impressions."

He shook his head. "You are certainly one to call out another on pride and prejudices, Miss Bennet. You have done little to hide your dislike for me from the moment we met."

Her eyes widened. "Perhaps it was because you told Mr. Bingley the night of the reception to welcome guests aboard that it would be a long and tedious three weeks with nary a handsome woman among the group, and none of sparkling wit or conversational abilities. You were looking directly at me as you spoke the insult, Mr. Darcy."

He flinched, looking uneasy for the first time that she could recall, other than when he was in social situations. "You heard that? But how? I was across the room."

Lizzy managed a small smile. "We had a gardener with a deaf son when I was a child. Wesley and I were friends, so when his master came to Longbourn to teach him how to read lips, I participated in the lessons as well. It has proven to be a most useful skill, though I have occasionally overheard words no one should."

His expression softened slightly. "I apologize for that comment, Miss Bennet. I was out of sorts and feeling ill that evening. I confess, I am not much for sailing, and seasickness had gotten the better of me. Charles was encouraging me to mingle and get acquainted with my fellow passengers, but I literally had no stomach for it. I spoke harshly and out of turn, irritated with him far more than the caliber of any company that might be aboard."

She cocked her brow, still skeptical. "You hold yourself aloof from everyone, Mr. Darcy. Perhaps you regret expressing your opinion so vehemently where I was able to discern it, but I doubt it changes your assessment."

He shrugged a shoulder. "I suppose it does not matter. I am

unlikely to change your opinion of me."

"Likewise, I am certain. I believe Mr. Bingley said once your good opinion is lost, it can never be regained. However, I do ask you to look upon my sister with new eyes and reconsider what judgments you have drawn against her. She is a kind woman, and she would be a good partner for Mr. Bingley if his affections are inclined in that direction."

He frowned. "Unfortunately, I suspect they are. If you will allow me to be blunt, Miss Bennet?"

She steeled herself as she squared her shoulders. "Please do, Mr. Darcy. There is a time and place for polite dancing around words, and there is a time for dispensing with the mincing of them."

"Your sister has no connections. I have not yet met the rest of your family, but your mother sounds dreadfully embarrassing. Any man who tied himself to the Bennets would be a disadvantaged fool. Charles is in a good position, but he is still vulnerable to the whims of society, and his business is successful based on connections he forges. To marry someone like Miss Bennet, who is not an heiress or particularly socially accomplished, would be a mistake."

Her lips tightened, and she reminded herself she had invited him to be blunt with his version of the truth. "I cannot deny anything you have said, but I still entreat you to look beyond your perceptions to see how the two of them feel about each other. Perhaps my sister is not the best match from a pragmatic viewpoint, but if she makes Mr. Bingley happy and vice versa, should that not be enough?"

He smirked. "What a naïve young woman you are. I know you did not grow up among the *ton*, so you likely do not understand full expectations, or just what social suicide it would be for a man of Mr. Bingley's or my standing to take a bride such as you…your sister."

She frowned at the words. "It is most fortunate for you that no one is asking you to take a Bennet as a bride, Mr. Darcy. You must concede you can hardly dictate the direction of Mr. Bingley's heart."

"No, indeed I cannot, or he would have already ended this unsuitable association with Miss Bennet. I can do my best to sway him toward seeing sense and reason though, and to point out the young lady in question seems little more than a fortune hunter."

Lizzy was pushed beyond the bounds of endurance. Before she

could think better of it, her hand snaked out and collided with Darcy's cheek with a resounding slap. The sound would have been even harsher if she hadn't been wearing a glove. "You go too far in your assertions, Mr. Darcy."

He grasped her wrist as she started to step back, pulling her closer. He glared down at her, and his chest was heaving just as hard as hers in his obvious anger. She stared up at him, rage clouding her vision, but there was a disconcerting irregularity in her pulse that couldn't be purely from the surge of adrenaline. She couldn't identify what was affecting her so strongly as his hand gradually loosened on her wrist, his thumb sliding underneath the cuff of her glove to touch the palm of her hand.

Perhaps they would've stared at each other like that all night, locked in a stalemate. Lizzy thought there was an expectation, an air of something more to come, though she didn't know what. She was most relieved when Jane's voice broke the spell, calling out, "Lizzy, come at once. There are dolphins."

She jerked her hand away from Darcy's hold and rushed to her sister, relieved to be away from him and whatever strange enchantment had stolen over her for a moment. The bloody nerve of the man, decrying her sister, and likely her as well, as fortune hunters. Her only regret was not slapping him harder.

CHAPTER TWO

Fitzwilliam was miserable, his stomach clenching and twisting as the ship listed back and forth on heavy waves. The storm had taken them by surprise, and the captain had immediately sent all the passengers belowdecks to their cabins. He looked across the room where Charles slept peacefully, seemingly unaware of how the ship was rocking, and the ill effects it had on his stomach.

In an attempt to distract himself, and because his cheek still stung, he lifted a hand to touch the area where Miss Bennet had slapped him. He found himself chuckling at the memory, though there had been nothing funny about it at the time. He'd been just as angry as her, but now, as he looked back with the benefit of a few hours of perspective, he found some amusement in the incident.

She'd looked so enraged, and her fine eyes, already pretty, had become captivating. For a woman, she had a firm right hook as well, though she'd not punched him.

Her palm had connected with his face, and he was grateful she had worn a glove, because he would likely have a bruise rather than just some tenderness if she had not.

It was a surprise to see that hint of passion in her, sparked by her mother bear instincts to protect her sister. Perhaps he had been too blunt with his opinion, but he couldn't deny he'd wanted to generate just such a response. There was something invigorating about arguing with Miss Bennet. Though he was a man unaccustomed to anything but harmonious accord in his domestic relationships, he couldn't deny he enjoyed trading barbs with her. It was almost like a form of foreplay.

He froze at the thought, forcefully rejecting it. Miss Bennet was entirely unsuitable, no matter what physical response she might engender within him. He might want to bend her over the rail and kiss her senseless, but he was in control of himself enough not to do so. She was eminently unsuitable for a wife, but she was far too respectable to make a mistress.

Fitzwilliam had never been one for keeping a mistress anyway. There was something sordid about the exchange of sex for money that bothered him. He was practical enough to understand why some women engaged in the practice, securing a better future than they would've had as serving girls, governesses, or companions. He could certainly see why a woman would choose to have one benefactor over many, and he wasn't so prudish that he didn't understand men and women both had needs of a sexual nature, but it was an arrangement that had never suited him.

It was only when he found himself contemplating the idea of approaching Lizzy with such an offer last week that he had realized the depths of his attraction to her.

He'd done his best to fight it every step of the way, but he had not yet managed to conquer the weakness. Since he was never going to enjoy the charms of holding Miss Bennet in his arms, it was a distant second to settle for trading witticisms and caustic comments.

He was distracted from his thoughts when the ship heaved particularly hard, and there was a cracking sound above. Darcy reached for the chamber pot, emptying the contents of his stomach before he rolled out of the berth and stood up. He walked over to Charles, shaking his friend on the shoulder. "Wake up, Charles. I think something is wrong."

Charles's eyes snapped open, and he looked instantly alarmed. "Is it Miss Jane?"

Fitzwilliam would've been more annoyed with his friend's first thoughts being for Miss Jane if he wasn't wondering similarly about the safety and state of Miss Elizabeth at the time. "I do not know. I heard a cracking sound from above, and I think it bodes ill."

"We must check on them then." Charles leapt out of bed, rushing to the dressing screen in the corner and emerging in record time wearing a shirt, breeches, and a waistcoat. He had not bothered with a cravat or jacket, and Fitzwilliam was in a similar state of dishabille, but it seemed unwise to take extra time to dress the part of the gentleman at the moment.

They departed their cabin together, walking rapidly down the hall. The Bennet sisters were at the end, tucked into what had likely been the cheapest cabin available, since it offered no view.

Fitzwilliam knocked firmly on the door, and it opened a moment later. Lizzy was in her nightdress and dressing gown. She seemed embarrassed when he stared at her, but she didn't look away or close the door. "Do either of you know what that sound was, Mr.

Bingley?" Oddly enough, though she asked Charles, her gaze was still locked with Fitzwilliam's. She had the good grace to flush a little, and he supposed she was recalling how violently she had reacted to his statement earlier.

"We do not, but we intend to find out." Fitzwilliam did his best to ignore his stomach churning with nausea from the rough rocking of the boat. He was thankful he had emptied the contents into the chamber pot, so there was nothing left to bring up, though the urge to do so remained.

"We should come with you," said Jane briskly, peering from

behind Lizzy. Unlike her sister, she was fully dressed.

"I do not think that is wise, Miss Jane," said Charles. "It could be rough up there, or perhaps dangerous."

"I would rather know if there is danger instead of hiding here in the cabin," said Jane.

"Quite right," said Lizzy.

Fitzwilliam reluctantly admired the spunk of both sisters. He could hardly imagine Miss Bingley or even his dear sister Georgiana having the same kind of fortitude. They would've locked themselves in the cabin and deferred to the gentlemen's judgment of whether further action must be taken.

Not bothering to argue with the sisters, he started walking forward. Charles apparently had realized it was futile as well, and he followed behind them, with the two women between them.

They were not the only passengers investigating the sound that had woken them, along with making the ship list violently left and then right again. Lizzy started to fall forward, her hand touching his lower back for a moment as she braced herself. With concern, he turned to face her. "You are well, Miss Bennet?"

She shrugged a shoulder. "I suppose. The sea is dreadfully rough this evening."

Fitzwilliam nodded, resisting the urge to offer an arm to steady her. He was certain she would reject such an innocent gesture prompted solely from decency. It had nothing to do with wanting to feel her skin close to his, while knowing she was likely only wearing two layers of clothing. His breeches grew uncomfortably tight for a moment at the thought, but the tossing of the ocean soon distracted him again.

They followed the line of passengers abovedeck, and it was far worse than Fitzwilliam had expected. Stepping up, he reached out a hand to assist Lizzy, and she actually took it without protest.

Once he was assured she was secure, he held out a hand to Miss Jane, offering her similar assistance. When Charles joined them a moment later, he stood behind Jane, his hands on her hips to help steady her. It was an inappropriate position and inadequate distance between them, but Fitzwilliam was far more concerned about what was happening around them than he was about matters of propriety, or how close his friend was getting to the unacceptable Miss Jane.

They had lost the mast. No wonder the ship was tossing about so fitfully, and as three frantic men ran by, Fitzwilliam heard one of them saying they needed to launch the lifeboats.

Alarmed by that, he looked around until he spotted the captain, who was wrestling with the wheel. He rushed over to him, darting through the crowd and doing his best not to fall on the slippery deck, though he skidded once and almost rammed into another passenger.

When he reached Captain Isaiah, he said, "How bad is it, Captain?"

The elder man cursed and heaved against the wheel. "'Tis bad enough, Mr. Darcy. Lightning took the mast, and as it did so, it damaged a portion of the hull while falling. The ship is taking on water, and 'tis such a prodigious amount there is no way we can repair the breach. We must abandon ship."

Fitzwilliam turned back toward his friend and the Bennet sisters, only to realize he'd lost them in the crowd. He looked around, moving through the other frantic passengers, who were lining up for the lifeboats. Word must've quickly circulated they had to abandon ship.

He caught sight of Lizzy then, eyes wide with shock when he saw her darting below-deck again. She didn't seem like the type who might cower in her state room, hoping to ignore the problem, and he darted after her, wondering at her foolishness. "Miss Bennet, come back." The strong wind and driving rain stole his words before she ever had hope of hearing them, and he plunged after her down the stairs.

He found her a moment later, entering the cabin she shared with Miss Jane. He stood in the doorway, staring at her in shock. "Whatever are you doing, woman? We must abandon ship. The captain has given the order."

"I know. I read his lips as you spoke to him." She didn't look up at him as she continued to frantically search her trunk.

She had garments in one hand, and he shook his head. "Surely you did not come back here for clothes?"

"No, but I might as well take some while I am here. Oh, where is it?" She sounded aggrieved.

He moved closer, realizing she was panicking, but it didn't seem to be from the storm. "For what are you searching? Perhaps I can help you find it, and we can get to safety sooner."

"My father's favorite book. He left me a letter in there, written when he knew he was going to die. I have never read it, so I must find it. Do you see?"

He frowned in confusion. "Why

have you not read it?" As he asked, he turned to the nightstand nearest him to open the drawer, looking for a book but turning up nothing.

"He said I must read it when I am certain I am in love. It has remained sealed, and so I have had no opportunity to do so, because I have not felt love. They were practically his dying words to me, Mr. Darcy."

He was about to insist she was going to have to give up the letter anyway, prepared to carry her out of the cabin if required, when she let out a cry of relief. She must've found what she sought, and she grasped the book, opening it long enough to ensure there was something inside.

He saw an envelope tucked into it before she secured it in a bag she took from a hook on the wall. It was an oilskin, and he hoped it would provide some protection for her treasured possession, especially since she was foolish enough to risk her life—and his— to retrieve it.

As soon as it was in the bag, he grasped her wrist and rushed her out of the room. He didn't wait for her to catch up, and when she slowed a little, he looked down and saw she was wearing no shoes. With a sigh of impatience, and some care for her feet due to the rough splintering of the wood, he bent down and lifted her, placing her over his shoulder.

He expected her to howl in outrage, but all she did was cling to him, her hands wrapped around his waist from behind. For a moment, he was sidetracked by just how close her thumb was to his manhood, but there was no time to think such improper thoughts.

He rushed them abovedeck again, heading toward the dwindling line for lifeboats. They were in luck, managing to secure spots on one of the last ones launched, along with three other passengers.

It was a rough drop into the water, and Lizzy cried out with shock, surprising Fitzwilliam when she clung to him for a moment. He wrapped his arms around her, a reassuring presence while taking comfort in having her with him.

He held her like that for more than an hour, as the small boat was tossed about by the waves. There were oars, but there was no point in trying to wield them at the moment. They would be no match for the strength of the sea. He could only hope they weren't washed away.

As if the thought had brought the action, a wave suddenly broke over them, tipping over the boat and sending the occupants into the water. She stiffened, and he clung to her for a moment before realizing she was pulling away to swim. She seemed to be competent, but he kept hold of the hem of her dressing gown to ensure he didn't lose her as they swam to the surface.

When they broke through a moment later, the rain was still drenching them, but it was safe to take a deep breath. He was certain Lizzy did the same, though he couldn't hear anything over the crash of the storm.

It was difficult to see anything in the dark water, and there was little moon in the sky to provide illumination. Fortunately, a crack of thunder, followed by lightning, illuminated the area long enough for him to see the lifeboat floating nearby. It was upside down, but he directed Lizzy toward it, guessing she had seen its location as well.

Together, they managed to tip it over and upright, and though it had some water in the bottom, he thought they could still float. He assisted her in before dragging himself into it as well, and then he looked around, hoping to find the other three who'd shared the boat with them.

At first, there was no sign, but

when another flash of lightning streaked the sky, he saw a hand sticking up as someone struggled to break the surface. He leaned over as far as he dared, conscious of Lizzy grabbing hold of his waist to steady him, and he grasped the hand to pull the young woman free from the ocean, dragging her back into the lifeboat.

She had a nasty gash on her head, and he worried about her, but he was preoccupied looking for the other two. A moment later, the boat tipped to the side, and he looked over to see a young man pulling himself out of the water. He landed in the water at the bottom of the boat, dragging in deep lungsful of air for a long moment.

He grimaced when he saw the piece of wood sticking out the young man's side. He looked at Lizzy as lightning flashed again, seeing similar concern in her gaze when it lit up the wound well enough for them to tell it was dreadful.

"Where is the other passenger?" called the young lady, seeming frantic. She was holding her head and wincing.

Fitzwilliam shook his head as he looked around. "I do not see her." It was too dangerous to jump from the lifeboat and swim, hoping to find the fifth person who'd been in there with them. He couldn't help thinking that if Lizzy were the one in the water, he would've taken the risk, but he held back for a stranger.

He couldn't explain why she drew him, but it seemed vitally important to protect Lizzy above anyone else, and though that was an uncomfortable thought, he didn't shy away from it. They were in mortal peril, and if he could help Lizzy in any fashion, he was prepared to sacrifice anyone else who was a stranger to do so.

They continued to search as they were subjected to the mercy of the storm, since the oars were gone now, but the fifth passenger never reappeared. Fitzwilliam could only assume the woman had gone to her death in the deep below. He shuddered at the thought, glancing at Lizzy again when lightning lit the sky, vowing she would not suffer such a fate.

***

He'd fallen asleep cold and miserable, but now Fitzwilliam woke hot and miserable. He looked up balefully at the sky, which was full of sun beaming down on them, with no shelter in sight. He glanced over to find Lizzy staring out at the water with a pensive expression.

As though she sensed his gaze

upon her, she turned to look at him, and their eyes met for a moment. She nibbled on her lower lip, her anxiety obvious. "I do not know when the storm ended, but it is as though it never happened, is it not?" She sounded shocked by the idea.

Fitzwilliam looked around, evaluating the sea. It seemed as placid as the day they'd set sail, but that was still enough to make the boat move more than his stomach liked. He saw no debris strewn around them, and he wondered how far they had drifted from the shipwreck. "Indeed." Abruptly recalling they shared the space with other passengers, he turned to look at them.

The young woman appeared to be asleep, but it was immediately obvious the young man, who still laid at the bottom of the boat, was gone. His body was pale and stiff, and Darcy winced as he leaned forward, alarmed by the amount of blood around the young man. It was enough to turn the water in the bottom of the boat pink, and he looked up when she gasped.

"He is dead, is he not, Mr. Darcy?" Her eyes were wide with horror.

He nodded. "I am afraid so. There was nothing we could have done for him anyway, Miss

Bennet."

She closed her eyes. "Still, he died alone from that trauma with none of us holding his hand or asking about him. How remiss of us."

Darcy tamped down a surge of guilt. "You are right. We were remiss, but the circumstances were, and continue to be, dreadful. It was all we could do to get through the storm." He eyed the young man before reaching down, opening his jacket.

Lizzy looked at him. "Whatever are you doing, Mr. Darcy?" She sounded scandalized, as though she suspected he was about to pick over the possessions of the departed young man.

He scowled up at her. "I am hoping he carries some sort of identification, Miss Bennet." It would provide some closure to his family—assuming the rest of them were rescued and could provide the information about the young man.

Searching through his pockets revealed a folded bank draft with his name on it, along with the balance revealing he had one hundred and two pounds to his name. Apparently, he had decided to start over in America.

Darcy was sad for the young man as he folded Mr. Pennyworth's bank draft and put it in his pants pocket, abruptly realizing he wore no jacket, cravat, or waistcoat. He tried not to be embarrassed by his current state lacking propriety. "I am afraid I must do something unpleasant, Miss Bennet."

She was looking at him with concern. "What is that, Mr. Darcy?"

"I must heave his body overboard."

She scowled. "You cannot without so much as a Christian burial."

His mouth tightened. "I do not enjoy the prospect either, but it is unhealthy to leave the dead body on the boat with us. We will say a prayer for him, and we know his name, so we can pass it along to his relatives."

After a second, she looked resigned as she nodded. "Yes, I suppose it must be done. What is his name, sir?"

"Harry Pennyworth." As Darcy spoke his name, he lifted the legs. He anticipated handling the grim business in two stages, first getting the legs over the side of the boat before moving around to try to lift the rest of the man into the water. It surprised him when Lizzy leaned forward and lifted the man's shoulders, obviously straining with the exertion, but together, they managed to lift him up and over the side of the boat, gently dropping him into the water.

"Farewell, Mr. Pennyworth. I hope your afterlife is happier than this one." Lizzy said a prayer for him.

Darcy muttered, "Amen," when she had finished.

They both turned their attention to the woman sharing the space with them after that, realizing she'd still not roused. Darcy recalled she had a fierce head injury, and he leaned forward as Lizzy did the same. Their heads almost collided before he pulled back, and she gave an awkward laugh. "I apologize, Mr.

Darcy. We apparently had the same thought at the same time."

He nodded, not verbally responding. He was unsettled they had similar thought processes. He wanted nothing in common with her, and thus far, he had seemed to have his wish. She was most improper, and she would never suit him—so why could he not stop thinking about her?

Darcy waited for Lizzy to reach out and touch the woman's shoulder. She shook her gently, but there was no response. Lizzy pulled lightly on her, and the woman slumped forward before falling onto her back as Lizzy caught her. She was breathing, but she showed no sign of awareness.

Darcy leaned forward, pressing a hand under her nose to ensure she was inhaling and exhaling, and she was, but he thought more slowly than normal. He looked up as Lizzy took her wrist, feeling for a pulse.

She frowned. "She is alive, but I think her heart is beating weakly."

Looking at the gash across her temple, he realized how deep it was. He could see part of her skull. He had no idea if she had sustained it before the lifeboat capsized or during the evacuation, but it was dreadfully swollen.

He reached over to peel up one of her eyelids and then the other, finding one pupil was far larger than the other. He was not medically trained in any way, but he suspected that was a bad sign. "I do not know that she will awaken, Miss Bennet. All we can do is try to make her comfortable if we can."

She looked around, her thoughts on the matter clear. "How will we do that, Mr. Darcy? We have no food or water, or even any shade."

He pressed his lips together bleakly. "I do not have any answers for you, Miss Bennet. I have never been in such a situation either."

Surprisingly, her expression

softened as she nodded. "Of course, Mr. Darcy. I did not mean to imply you did, or you should know all the answers. I am frustrated and frightened, I suppose."

He nodded. "As am I, Miss Bennet."

He looked away when he realized she was starting to remove her night rail. He wondered if it was because it was hot, or if she had another purpose. It soon became obvious she was using it to drape over the unconscious woman sprawled between them.

He wanted to suggest she keep it for her own complexion instead, but he knew she would not be so selfish to do so. From what he'd observed of her, though she was completely unsuitable to be his bride, she seemed to be a compassionate woman, and she obviously cared greatly for her sister, and apparently, that care extended to strangers as well.

Why not him? It was a strange, sullen thought, and he felt ridiculous as it came to him. They had rubbed each other wrong from the start, and as the very real possibility he might be stranded alone with her until rescue sank in, his stomach heaved again. It wasn't the rocking of the boat this time. It was a strange mix of dread and anticipation, and he clenched his hands into fists.

When he realized they might not be rescued, and this situation could last for the rest of their short lives, true nausea surged in him, and he bent over the boat to release the contents of his stomach. When he sat back, he felt weak, both physically and emotionally, though he saw only care and concern on Lizzy's face. He still flushed with the revelation of his vulnerability, and he did his best to steer the subject away from what he'd just done. "I do hope Charles and Miss Jane made it to safety as well."

She looked around for a moment. "So do I. We are not yet

safe, but I think I see land over the horizon." She pointed in the direction as she spoke.

He looked that way, agreeing he saw something that could be an island. The question was, could they reach it in time, especially with their oars gone? They would be at the mercy of the ocean, and there was a chance it would drift them in the right direction. If not, it could take them completely the wrong way, and they would likely starve to death or die of dehydration before encountering more land or a rescue party.

"I am certain Mr. Bingley will look out for Jane."

He frowned. "Why are you sure

they are together?" The thought left him uneasy.

She glared at him, apparently taking issue with his tone. "Why are you sure they are not, Mr. Darcy? Mr. Bingley was beside my sister the entire time I was abovedeck, before realizing I had to get Papa's letter."

He shook his head. "That was a bit of foolishness."

She glared at him. "And yet you followed me. What does that say about you, Mr. Darcy?"

"I too am a fool, Miss Bennet." He refused to contemplate what else it might say about him, like how much the thought of losing her eviscerated him, and how he'd plunged after her in a panic, intent on saving her even though he hadn't understood the circumstances, or what she was after.

Grudgingly, he wondered if Charles felt the same way for Miss Jane. If so, the two of them were likely together, and if that happened, he could easily envision a scenario where his friend foolishly offered for Miss Jane, despite all her shortcomings.

He was never going to be so foolish, of course. He had a firm handle on his inappropriate attraction to Miss Elizabeth Bennet, and nothing would sway him from the prudence of avoiding any further entanglement with her.

CHAPTER THREE

Luck must've been with them, because the wind whipped up that day and pushed them closer to the island. Lizzy was hopeful they would reach it before nightfall, but it wasn't to be. The wind stopped, and they seemed to be at a standstill again for a time, though they were gently bobbing along.

She was worried they were getting out of range of the island, and Mr. Darcy seemed equally tense. Without a light source, they could only rely on the stars and the moonlight above them, and though there was a little more moon this evening, it was still inadequate for their needs.

Lizzy shivered, cold all over again. She had the dress she'd grabbed from her trunk, using it to protect the book, but there was no way she could change. Her clothes had at least dried in the hot sunlight, but now they felt stiff and itchy, and she kept scratching discreetly.

"Whatever is the matter?" asked

Mr. Darcy after a long moment, sounding impatient.

Lizzy's scratching must be rocking the boat. "I apologize, but I itch. My clothes did not dry well."

His tone was softer when he replied, though the darkness made it impossible to read his expression. "I can relate to that. Wool is dreadfully uncomfortable after it has gotten wet and dried in such a fashion."

She winced in sympathy, imagining how much warmer he had been than her during the day with his wool breeches. On the other hand, they provided more warmth for him now. She shivered again, shocked when he reached out for her hand. He tugged her forward, and she said, "Whatever are you doing?"

"It seems prudent to share body heat."

Lizzy knew she should protest, but she was dreadfully cold now that the sun had set, so she allowed him to pull her toward him, carefully navigating around the young woman who had still not regained consciousness, though she hadn't passed away either. The poor dear was stuck in some state of limbo, and Lizzy sympathized. She and Darcy were alert, but they were also stuck in limbo. If they could reach the island, they stood a chance of survival, but if not, they would die out here.

Her throat was also scratchy, terribly so, and she longed for water. "It is terribly unfair, Mr. Darcy." She scooched a little, leaning back against him to get more comfortable. She fit against him with odd perfection, as though his arms had been made to cradle her. She was disquieted by the thought and tried to reject it.

"Our circumstances, Miss Bennet?"

She nodded. "Those too, but I was referring to being surrounded by water, being dreadfully thirsty, and yet unable to drink."

"I concur." His voice sounded as hoarse as hers. "It is most unfair. Perhaps there will be fresh water on the island. If not, maybe we can figure out a way to remove some of the salinity. I read a fascinating article in a travel journal recently about a man who managed to do just that while he was on expedition."

"You read such things?" Lizzy's eyes widened in the darkness, finding it a difficult prospect to believe. Mr. Darcy seemed so staid and proper that she could not imagine him being the type to read about others' adventures, let alone have one of his own.

"My sister has a fondness for

such things. She is also a fan of the penny dreadfuls and the penny dramas. We often read together."

"Oh. Then it is hardly surprising."

He stiffened. "I feel like I am being insulted in some fashion, Miss Bennet."

She grimaced. "I did not mean it that way, Mr. Darcy. I simply meant I am unsurprised to learn you are reading such material for your sister and not for your sake."

"Indeed?" He sounded cool. "Who do you think introduced Miss Georgiana to the topic to start with, Miss Bennet?" His words were terse.

She squirmed slightly, which only reminded her of how tightly she was pressed against Mr. Darcy, his delicious body warmth suffusing her own to take off the chill she'd experienced for the last hour. "I apologize. I suppose I made certain assumptions. You do not seem like a man who craves adventure."

He gave a dark chuckle. "I was quite a bit more adventurous as a young man, but I confess, I could do well without this adventure. If I did not allow Charles to persuade me into this foolishness, I would not be here."

Lizzy relaxed further against him. "Perhaps, but I am rather glad you are, Mr. Darcy." The darkness must have given her courage to make the admission. "I would not like to be alone in this, and I am not confident I would have reached a lifeboat without your assistance."

"In that case, allow me to amend my statement. I find it wretched that we are in such circumstances, but I am happy I was able to be of any assistance whatsoever." His lips brushed against her ear when he said the words, making her shiver. "You are still cold?"

She nodded quickly, too embarrassed to admit the shiver had come from an entirely different reason. She no longer felt cold. Instead, she was burning up with a different kind of fever, one she'd never had before. Her body felt more sensitive, and there was an ache between her thighs she couldn't explain as he shifted enough to pull her closer, turning her to face him so she was straddling his lap.

She was abruptly aware of the bulge there, and she quickly slammed her eyes shut and leaned against his chest, pretending she was desperate for sleep. Instead, she was desperate to pretend the situation wasn't occurring. Mr. Darcy seemed to be aroused for *her*, and though she told herself that was likely just a normal physical response, and any man would react the same to any young woman on his lap, there was a part of her thrilled with the idea.

The reality of her situation soon washed away any excitement from the illicit embrace. Lizzy was daring and curious, but realizing she might die at any moment, or that the ocean could sweep them away from the island before they got close enough to swim for it, had a dampening effect on even the most ardent libido.

She clung to him, trembling this time from fear rather than anything else as his arms held her securely. As afraid as she was, she was certain she would've been ten times more terrified if Mr. Darcy hadn't been there to offer comfort in the moment.

CHAPTER FOUR

Fitzwilliam woke with the first light of dawn, and when he looked down, he found Lizzy still sprawled across his lap, sleeping against him. His gaze moved to the woman who shared the space with them, and he was certain she had passed. Her skin was pale, and when he reached forward, it was waxy and cool to the touch. He let out a sigh of regret at the loss of life before turning his attention to Lizzy. "Miss Bennet, you need to wake now."

Her eyes opened slowly, and she smiled up at him with warmth that made his stomach curl in a delightful fashion. Only heavier matters distracted him from the urge to bend his head and kiss her. "Our fellow survivor is no more."

Sleep cleared from her eyes, and she blinked as she moved back abruptly, obviously realizing she'd fallen asleep in his arms and remained there for the night. If she was embarrassed, she didn't reveal it when she focused her attention on the young woman.

They looked through her things, but unlike for poor Mr. Pennyworth, they found no identification. She was wearing a simple cross with an inscription on the back that read: *"Eternally yours, N."* Lizzy removed it from her and placed it in her bag, hoping it might help identify the woman at some point.

She seemed to refuse the idea they might not be rescued, and Fitzwilliam tried not to dwell on it, since the island was tantalizingly close now. It was still too far away for him to feel comfortable trying to swim for it, but if the boat seemed like it would take them the wrong direction, and they couldn't overcome the ocean currents, he was confident that within a few hours, they would be close enough to make the attempt safe. There was reassurance in that, as long as the boat stayed the course for those remaining hours.

Together, they lifted the woman's body over the side of the boat, once more saying a prayer for her. Lizzy seemed to be in a dark mood. "If you outlive me, Mr. Darcy, please do not say the Lord's prayer when you drop me into the ocean. I do not find comfort in it. It is a stark reminder of what trials and tribulations one might face before reaching the next life."

His lips firmed. "I shall not recite the prayer, and you shall never be in that position. You are going to survive this, Lizzy. We both are."

She blinked. "You have used my first name."

He flushed. "I apologize. I was impassioned by the moment."

She smiled. "It seems rather ridiculous to be worried about such things, does it not, Mr. Darcy?"

He shrugged. "At the moment, it does. You may call me by my first name if you would like, Miss Elizabeth?"

She smiled. "Lizzy is fine, Mr.

Darcy, but I do not know your first name."

He laughed, a startled sound that made her jump in reaction. "No, I do not suppose you do. Charles fondly calls me Darcy, as do many of my acquaintances. Perhaps it is because they know I do not like my first name as well."

She tipped her head slightly. "Now you have me dreadfully curious, Mr. Darcy. Whatever is it?"

His lips twitched, enjoying her amusement and the way it distracted her from reality. "Perhaps I shall make you guess, Lizzy."

She tipped her head. "That is a

fine idea, Mr. Darcy. It will surely occupy the time until we are close enough to the island to swim for it."

He frowned slightly, realizing she wasn't as distracted as he'd hoped. Of course, she wasn't. She was an intelligent woman, and she recognized the peril of their situation, even if she was willing to indulge in a light bit of play to divert them from that. "What is your best guess?"

"Bartholomew."

He grimaced, finding that name even more objectionable than his own. "Decidedly not."

"Horatio?"

He shook his head. "My father

had a dear friend named Horatio, who was a giant bear of a man. He did enjoy his sporting and drink, much to his detriment. He combined the two one day. He was quite inebriated when he went out hunting for grouse and stumbled off a cliff."

She winced. "How horrible."

"Indeed. That is not my name though."

"James?" He shook his head. "William?"

He grinned. "You are close. Perhaps a clue?" At her eager nod, he said, "It starts with an F."

She frowned. "I am afraid I can think of no name that starts with F and contains William."

He grimaced. "Indeed, and that is part of the reason I so dislike the name. It is too unusual. The cursed moniker is Fitzwilliam, though my close acquaintances often call me Darcy, and my sister calls me Will."

Lizzy nodded. "I see. Which would you prefer I use, Mr. Darcy?"

There was a lump in his throat as he imagined her saying the diminutive his sister always used for him. Georgiana spoke it with a caring note, and he wondered how it would sound coming from Lizzy in such a fashion. "Will shall do fine, Lizzy."

"Very well, Will." She smiled at

him. "How much longer do you think it will be before we can swim for the island if the boat isn't going to take us there?"

He looked at the sky and then at the island. "I do not know, but hopefully only a few hours. It would be better if we can keep the boat, but if not, I think we will soon be within a safe distance to swim."

***

They were unable to keep the boat in the end. The wind whipped up and started pulling them the other direction, so together, they jumped into the ocean and swam. He admired how strong a swimmer Lizzy was as they reached the island thirty minutes later, both breathing heavily before collapsing onto the wet sand. He glanced over at her, waiting until he could catch a breath before he said, "I am surprised how well you swim. Most ladies of my acquaintance do not possess such a skill."

Her lips twitched, though she was still obviously trying to get a deep breath. "I have no doubt the ladies of your acquaintance are quite accomplished in different tasks, including drawing, modern languages, and all the rules of decorum and etiquette." Said like that, it managed to sound almost insulting.

He shrugged. "Perhaps, but swimming is certainly not among them."

She smiled. "Growing up in the country has many advantages, including our own spring. My sisters and I spent many summers in the water before Mama deemed us too old for such things."

His lips twitched. "Even after your mother forbade you, you still swam upon occasion?"

She seemed unrepentant as she rolled onto her side to face him. "I swam every chance I got, Will. It is something I truly enjoy, and I have not a bit of regret for defying her, since it likely saved my life."

He nodded, leaving it unspoken

that it might've saved his as well. He never would have left her behind, but trying to tow her with him across the distance might've been enough to leave them both drowning before they could ever reach land.

Sometime later, the water started to wash over them, and it roused Fitzwilliam enough to sit up. He looked at Lizzy, who was doing the same. "I suppose we should see what is available to us, and how we can survive on this place."

She nodded, licking her dry lips. "I hope there is water."

"If you would like to make yourself comfortable in the shade,

I shall search for it."

"I can come with you."

He waved a hand. "You should rest." No doubt, as a lady, she'd exceeded her strength by vast margins. Even Fitzwilliam was feeling depleted, but it was his duty as the man to look after her and ensure she had water if he could find it.

Fitzwilliam moved into the interior of the island, unsurprised to find a wild jungle. He heard animals ahead of him, though they fell silent each time he approached, likely sensing an interloper in their midst and wanted to hide their presence. He felt similarly, hoping any life on the island was small and shy, wishing to stay away from them rather than be aggressive. Without even a weapon, an animal attacking was a frightening prospect.

Though his energy was flagging, Darcy pushed on, walking until he found a freshwater source a couple of kilometers later. There were no animals around, and the water looked clean and cool. He could clearly see the stones in the shallow end. He had no container with which to retrieve it, so he looked around before finding a section of bark he thought might hold enough to be worth the trip back. He quenched his thirst and washed the vessel as thoroughly as he could before filling it with water. Holding it carefully, he slowly returned to where he'd left Lizzy on the beach.

CHAPTER FIVE

Lizzy had hardly sat inactive on the beach, and she wasn't likely to. Her survival depended on what they could do with the situation as much as Mr. Darcy's... Will's, she corrected herself. Instead of idling away her time like she was at a garden party, she started collecting materials to build two shelters.

She was in the process of arranging them when Mr. Darcy returned bearing the bark of a log full of water. He set it down carefully, and she rushed forward to slake her thirst before using a bit to wash off her face and hands. "I should very much like to go swimming in this water and get off the sticky salt feeling, Mr. Darcy."

"Will," he corrected. "I am certain that can be arranged. I did not see anything overtly threatening on my way to discovering it." He looked at the pile of rocks, bark, twigs, and leaves she'd assembled. "What is all this?"

"We shall need shelters, so I was starting on them."

He nodded. "I have a bold suggestion, Lizzy."

She arched a brow. "What is it?"

"Rather than making two smaller shelters, I think we should combine our efforts to make a sturdier one large enough for both of us. Would you find that acceptable?"

She bit her lip, seeing the wisdom despite the impropriety. After a moment, she shrugged. "It hardly matters, does it, Will? Whether we have separate shelters or share one, we are both alone on this island. I do not think anyone will ever know."

He nodded. "In that case, I shall get to work immediately."

She frowned. "And I shall help you."

He grimaced. "You should be resting."

She rolled her eyes. "If I should be, so should you, Mr. Darcy, but our shelter shall not build itself. We must work together and hasten the process."

He looked like he would protest, but after a moment, he nodded. "You are correct. We should combine our efforts."

***

Lizzy ached all over later that evening as she laid on the sand outside the shelter they had built.

It was a humble little structure, but it would do for now. Perhaps it would not survive a hurricane or strong wind and rain, but if they were here long enough to worry about it, they would fortify it further in future.

At the moment, she just wanted to rest, though she couldn't seem to bring herself to move from the fire to enter the shelter and lie down on the leaves forming a makeshift bed. When Mr. Darcy approached and handed her a coconut, she stared at it. "I have read about these, but I have never eaten one."

"Nor have I. I believe they are difficult to open." He looked around at the collection of rocks they hadn't used for the shelter, picking one with a suitably sharp edge. "I suppose we just break it open." As he said that, he smashed the coconut on the rock. It took three good, solid hits before a crack appeared, and water started to drip out. He quickly brought it to his mouth, catching what was leaking forth.

Lizzy was mesmerized by the sight of his throat working as he swallowed, and she had the strangest urge to lean forward and lick the residue of coconut water from his chin. She blinked, shocked at the idea and the way her body was suddenly warm in a way unattributable to the fire. She cleared her throat, saying, "I take it the taste must be pleasurable?"

His gaze met hers, smoldering. "Most pleasurable. I have never tasted anything quite like it." He handed her the cracked coconut, and Lizzy opened it the rest of the way to find there was still plenty of water inside, along with the meat. He cracked the one she'd held, and they spent the next several minutes eating and drinking in silence.

"That was most satisfying, but we must find other food sources. I suspect subsisting on coconut would not be healthy," said Lizzy.

"Probably not. Tomorrow, I

think I shall try to fashion a spear, if I can find a small enough rock with a sharp enough edge."

She frowned. "Why do you need a spear on this island, Mr. Darcy? I believe I heard monkeys chittering earlier, but they are quick and sly. I doubt we could catch one."

He grinned. "Likely not. I had a rather different task in mind. Have you heard of spearfishing?"

Lizzy shook her head, leaning back against the sand as he told her what he had read in a journal. She frowned with doubt. "It sounds dreadfully difficult."

"I suppose, but what else do we have to do around here?"

She smiled. "Yes, there is that." She barely stifled a yawn that swept over her. "I believe I am exhausted, Will."

"As am I, Lizzy." He stood up, coming over to offer her a hand out of the sand. When she stood up, he casually brushed sand off her nightdress. "I am surprised you did not wear your dress once we washed ashore."

She shrugged. "It is far too heavy for the hot work we were doing, Mr. Darcy."

"I assure you I shall be the soul of discretion and share this with no one"

She smiled. "That is assuming we ever see anyone to share it with." With those grim words, she nodded her head to him, went a few feet into the jungle to see to her nightly needs, and then returned to slide into the shelter a short time later.

Mr. Darcy was already there, lying atop the leaves they had spread on the sand. It was certainly not the most comfortable bed, but she was too exhausted from the ordeal and the physical activity of the day to spare much thought for comfort, and she was asleep almost as soon as her eyelids closed.

CHAPTER SIX

While Darcy busied himself making a spear the next morning, Lizzy recovered more materials from the jungle and driftwood from the beach to build a signal fire. If they kept their smaller fire burning—and they had every intention of doing so, since it had taken the two of them quite a long time to figure out how to start a spark yesterday when neither one of them had ever even lit a fire in a fireplace before—they could quickly light the bonfire to signal for help if they saw a ship approaching.

She looked up when Mr. Darcy cursed, shocked at his lapsed manners. "Is everything all right, Will?"

He looked at her, flushing. "My apologies, Lizzy. These blasted fish are far too difficult to spear. I suspect the article I read was full of distortions and contrivances."

Her lips twitched as she moved away from the bonfire, holding out her hand. "I should very much like to try."

With a frown, he passed it over to her. "It is difficult, I warn you."

She nodded. "I do enjoy a challenge." At first, she started out on the beach as he had been, but that seemed illogical to her. It took forever for fish to even come close, so she lifted her nightdress, her dress still in her satchel, and wrapped it around her waist. She ignored Darcy's indrawn breath as she plunged into the water, standing still for what felt like forever.

Her first few attempts ended ignobly, but she let out a cry of delight when the next time she tried, she speared a large fish. "I have one," she cried out with glee as she turned to face him, grasping the fish firmly by the gills. She squirmed at the sensation before he took it from her.

She expected him to be disgruntled, and he looked mildly displeased until he saw the fish. "Well done, Lizzy. I shall clean it if you would like to try to catch another?"

She nodded as she turned back to her task. "You know how to clean a fish, Mr. Darcy?"

"Indeed. I am quite adept at hunting and fishing. I have been doing so since before I can fully remember. Both my father and my uncle, the Earl of Matlock, were avid sportsmen. Uncle still does the occasional spot of hunting these days."

"It could prove quite useful for us then." Lizzy paused, holding her breath as a large fish swam by before darting back to her. When it was near a rock, she rushed forward, shoving the spear forcefully into it. She had a wince of regret for the poor thing as it flopped against the rock for a moment while she tugged loose the spear. The fish started to slip away, but she reached out and grabbed it, thankful it was slowed by its current condition. She tossed it on the beach to Darcy, who was currently busy stripping skin and fish guts from the first catch.

As she turned to walk toward him, deciding they had enough fish for the evening, she was unexpectedly overcome with arousal at the primitive sight before her. Right now, in just his breeches and boots, having shed his shirt sometime during the hot day, he looked nothing like the proud and disdainful scion of society she'd met the first night of the reception aboard the ship. Instead, he seemed savagely beautiful, and there was wildness in her heart urging her to join him.

Before she could talk herself out of it, Lizzy reached for the sharp rock he was using to cut the fish and used it to slice the side of her nightdress. When it was to her knee, she turned the makeshift knife to make another notch, ripping it widthwise as well. She felt much freer, and she ignored his look of shock as she sat down near him. "Show me how to skin this fish, Will."

He shook his head. "It is an unladylike task and quite disgusting, as you can see."

Lizzy nodded but affirmed her resolve by stiffening her shoulders. "I see that, but it is still a skill I desire to learn. I might need to know how to do it to take care of myself at some point."

With a grunt, he told her to find a sharp rock similar to the one he was using. When she returned, he had waited, though he'd finished filleting the first fish. He talked her through the process, and as she finished up a while later, handing over the fish that he wrapped in leaves and placed near the fire as he'd done with the first fillets, he said, "That shall never happen."

She frowned. "What do you mean?"

"You will not be alone to fend for yourself."

There was something in his voice, a tantalizing note that made it difficult not to believe him.

Lizzy firmed her shoulders anyway. "No one can be sure of that, Mr. Darcy, so it is wise that I learn to take care of myself." She frowned. "I do hope Jane is not in a similar situation. Mr. Bingley would surely look out for her, but I do not know that Jane could endure such hardship. Ever since she had scarlet fever as a child, her constitution is not as strong, and when cholera nearly knocked her flat almost three years ago, I fear she never quite recovered from that."

"I hope they are not stranded together on an island like us, deserted with just the two of them." His lips twisted. "Mr.

Bingley will assuredly find himself married at that point."

She glared at him. "My sister would be just as ruined, Mr. Darcy." She couldn't bring herself to call him Will at the moment.

He turned to her, arching a brow. "You really think so? She would not have the better advantage, having acquired a wealthy husband who is forced into a position to offer for her to avoid her ruin? I believe Charles would be the greater injured. Ruination can be beneficial for some."

She glared at him. "I am just as ruined as my sister in this situation, Mr. Darcy, and there is no benefit."

His eyes closed for a minute, and he heaved a sigh clearly full of regret. "Yes, I realize that. When we are rescued, I shall preserve your reputation by offering for you."

He was so reluctant and so burdened by the idea that Lizzy's mouth dropped open in shock, and for an instant, she had no words to express the depth of her outrage.

He continued, clearly unaware she wasn't feeling any gratitude for his sacrifice. "Of course, that would come with a generous settlement upon you and shouldering the responsibility for your family. Perhaps this is not the worst thing that has ever happened to you, Lizzy."

She struggled to breathe and control the urge to slap him. Her gloves were long gone, and she was certain she could leave a bruise if she tried this time, but the idea was disquieting. Lizzy was not particularly forceful or physical, except with this man.

Squeezing her hands into fists, she stood up and strode to the water, intent on removing the fish guts from her hands. "It will please you to know I would never marry you under any circumstances, Mr. Darcy. Indeed, I had not known you an hour before I couldn't imagine a man I would like less, and the idea of being tied to you for life is no joy."

He sounded shocked. "What choice would you have? We are compromised."

She turned back to glare at him as she scrubbed her hands. "I assure you I will never compromise about that, Mr. Darcy. Your fortune and your virtue are quite safe from me. I want no part of you or marriage to you."

With those words, she turned and strode down the beach, needing to get away from him. For the first time, she regretted she hadn't insisted on maintaining two smaller shelters. It would've at least given her the illusion of privacy to escape him for a while.

CHAPTER SEVEN

Fitzwilliam regretted his words, or at least how he'd delivered them. He had been making a magnanimous gesture, and her revilement of it was puzzling. How could she not benefit from such an arrangement as being Mrs. Fitzwilliam Darcy? How could he do anything less than decorum dictated, nay demanded, and offer for her hand if and when they were rescued?

The two of them were alone on this island, and with no chaperone, they could get up to all manner of impropriety. Society would insist on their marriage to preserve both their standings.

His breeches got tight at the thought of all the improprieties in which they might engage. He cleared his throat as he realized perhaps he wasn't as disadvantaged as he'd considered to start with. This opportunity gave him the perfect excuse to stop resisting his attraction to Lizzy and to claim her as his own.

Especially here, on this island, it

was a distant concept that she didn't have the right social standing and was burdened by such a family. No one among their acquaintance could blame either of them for finding comfort in each other as long as they were prepared to behave appropriately and fall in with societal expectations when they were rescued.

Indeed, Lizzy was practically his wife already, barring only the formalities…and the wedding night. He groaned as need tightened his groin, responding to the mental image of her sitting on him, taking his length inside her hot, slick core.

He banished the thought as much as he could, knowing he was no callow youth, and he refused to indulge in self-pleasure when there was a possibility she might catch him in the act. He could imagine nothing more humiliating, so he turned his attention back to preparing their fish.

He was unsurprised when she returned almost an hour later, this time with the sweet orange fruits in hand. Neither of them knew the name of it, but it was oval with red and orange skin and golden flesh, with a sweet, slightly tart taste. They had both discovered a liking for it the day before. She handed him two without speaking and took two for herself before sitting down near him. He passed her leaf-wrapped filets he'd kept warm near the fire, and she opened the packet without looking at him.

He cleared his throat. "My wording was unfortunate, Lizzy. I did not mean to imply it would be a great burden to marry you."

She looked up at him through narrowed eyes. "I suggest this is a conversation we do not revisit, Mr. Darcy."

He winced at the continued use of his surname. "Lizzy, will you please relent and call me Will? Let us talk this through. I did not mean to insult you. When the time comes to offer you for you, I shall do so gladly. We are practically already married, such as circumstances are arranged for us."

She scoffed. "We are anything but, Mr. Darcy. We have had very little impropriety between us, and it shall remain that way. Society will have no cause to insist on our marriage if we just explain—"

He laughed, a genuine belly laugh, though he hated her to think he was mocking her. "I do not wish to disillusion you, but you must know how naïve that sounds. Society will think what they wish, and they will always interpret actions in the most sordid way possible. Indeed, the only way to preserve either one of our reputations is for us to marry."

She shrugged a shoulder. "We will be going to America. No one there will know me, and they certainly shall not know about this incident. I see no reason why we would ever have to marry."

He gritted his teeth, wanting to continue to persuade her, but he was afraid it would just push her away rather than get her to concede to the necessity of their marriage. Now that he had embraced the idea, he was impatient for her to do the same, but he counseled himself to give her time and space. "Perhaps it will never be an issue then."

She nodded. "Undoubtedly."

He couldn't help wondering if it would be an issue if and when she capitulated to the attraction between them. If that led to a child, he would have to insist on marriage even if she were trying to be stubborn. No Darcy heir would be born out of wedlock, and he doubted even Lizzy was independent enough to try to insist otherwise.

***

Fitzwilliam did his best to maintain his patience over the next several days, behaving with care and concern, all with the goal of deepening their interactions. At first, she kept him at a distance, and though she called him Will, there was no sense that she meant it in a friendly or intimate way. It seemed to be a chore for her to say his name, but as he persisted, the days passing with frightful slowness due to lack of activity once they had secured food for each day, he could see her softening toward him.

When he fashioned a chessboard for them and retrieved shells of similar colors but different enough to be two sets of playing pieces, he saw the first signs of true softening in her. She smiled with pleasure, and they spent the rest of the day engaged in chess. She was a formidable opponent, and Fitzwilliam was surprised to lose more than he won. He might've been irked if it had been someone else, but Lizzy was so genuinely vibrant and intelligent that he couldn't find it in him to mind she could outwit him on several occasions.

He had a feeling she could completely undo him, and he was eager for that to happen. They had been on their island for a little more than a week when he admitted to himself he was in love with her. Perhaps he shouldn't have known her long enough, but between the time they'd spent here and on the ship, he'd fallen for her fine eyes, pert words, and womanly charms. He ached to possess her, though he was uncertain of her feelings for him.

That morning, she emerged from the shelter well past him, having overslept. He smiled at her as he presented a makeshift tray made from leaves adorned with bananas, coconut, and those orange fruits. "I have tried and failed my hand at fishing yet again, Lizzy, so it is incumbent upon you to save us once more."

She giggled as she took the plate of fruit and sat down on a rock. They had spent some time improving their shelter, including find two flat rocks and another larger one that worked as a crude table. She placed her makeshift plate on it now and started eating. "I shall attempt to catch fish after breakfast then."

"I shall be endeavoring to catch something else."

She looked up at him, clearly intrigued. "To what do you refer, Will?"

"Just this morning, I saw a wild boar when I was retrieving the bananas. Pork sounds quite lovely, does it not?"

She nodded, licking her lips with anticipation. "That would be most splendid, but are you certain it is safe? You do not have a musket."

His spine stiffened. "I beg your pardon, Miss Bennet, but I am certain I can handle taking on a boar with a spear."

She seemed on the verge of giggling. "It is true boar might not be quite as fast as fish."

"Impudent." With those words, he rushed toward her, and she giggled as she got to her feet and started running. Fitzwilliam caught up with her shortly, bringing her down to the sand. He tickled her until she was pink in the face and begging for him to stop. "Retract your insult, Miss Bennet," he said in a stiff tone, though he was unable to stifle his amusement.

She squirmed underneath him. "Fine. I retract the truth."

"You are an irredeemable chit." He continued to tickle her, realizing abruptly the way she was rubbing against him felt good in an entirely different way than just the camaraderie between them. His cock was growing heavy with need, and he ached to slide inside her.

Abruptly, he sat back, trying to control those urges. He was not opposed to anticipating their wedding vows, but he did not wish to rush Lizzy or make her think he wanted something corrupt from her and nothing permanent. "I shall accept your weak apology."

If she realized why he'd withdrawn abruptly, she gave no indication. She was grinning, appearing as carefree as ever. "I have every confidence you shall overtake the boar, Mr. Darcy." She winked at him. "A gentleman like you could do no less."

She got to her feet, brushing off the nightdress she wore. It was ragged around the edges now and had crept up to midthigh rather than knee-level. He knew she must take it off sometimes to wash in the water, and she'd been to swim in the freshwater a few times, as had he. They acted as lookouts for each other, ensuring no animals approached, and it took every ounce of strength he had not to turn around and peek at her as she bathed, but he had maintained gentlemanly behavior in that regard.

He set out shortly after, having spent a good part of the morning whittling a few new spears while waiting for Lizzy to awaken and present her with the bounty of fruit and the news he was going hunting.

He had never hunted wild boar, but he didn't expect it to be much different from deer, and he tracked it successfully until he had it penned in an area against the rocks jutting from the cliff face near the water. Up close, the boar was more fearsome than he'd expected, with wickedly sharp tusks, but he was determined to provide protein for himself and Lizzy. She had become good at spearing fish, but there were still far more meals of fruit than anything else, and he didn't want her to weaken. He didn't want to weaken either, since it was his duty to protect her.

He lunged forward with a spear, landing only a glancing blow on in the hind quarter of the boar. He pulled it back as the animal turned, screeching at him in rage.

Fitzwilliam had another spear ready to go, but the boar pushed right through it, running at him with great speed he had not expected. He scrambled up a nearby tree, but the tusk of the creature dug a deep furrow into his leg as it took a chunk of him while running by.

He cursed, looking down at the wound and wincing. He wasn't far from the waterhole, so he made his way there slowly, limping as he immersed his leg in the fresh water.

He looked up at the sound of movement through the jungle, grasping the spear he still held. He was afraid it was the boar coming back, perhaps determined to finish him off, but instead, Lizzy emerged from the undergrowth a moment later. She smiled at him at first until she realized there was a problem. "What is wrong?"

He looked away, flushing from the heat of embarrassment. "I am afraid the boar got the best of me."

She rushed toward him, uncaring he was submerged in the water. She leaned down, feeling his leg for herself, apparently not realizing she was perched on his thigh to do so. Having her heated flesh so close to his skin, with only the wool of his breeches he had cut off to above the knee and her nightdress separating them was enough to make him hard, and it temporarily took away the pain.

"You might need stitches."

"We do not have such supplies." He sighed. "I am sorry, Lizzy. I planned a different outcome."

She shrugged. "Animals are unpredictable. Let me help you up and back to our camp." She ignored his protest as she stood up, aiding him from the water and having him lean on her.

Fitzwilliam did his best to support most of his weight, but it was helpful to have her assistance. When they returned to their shelter a short time later, he collapsed onto the sand. He just wanted to rest and allow the wound to heal for a bit. He thought it would be a minor inconvenience. His pride stung far worse than his leg.

Chapter Eight

He was burning with fever. A little more than a day later, Lizzy was terrified Darcy was going to succumb to the infection raging through him. She did her best to keep his brow bathed with cool water, and she continuously cleaned the wound. She tried to keep him fed and hydrated, but she feared he was losing the battle.

She sat beside him that evening, holding his hand when he thrashed on his leaves, and she curled her hands around his. "You have to be okay, Will. I do not want to do this without you. I do not think I can. Please, fight for me." The idea of losing him was devastating, and Lizzy realized she had done the unthinkable. She'd fallen in love with a man who was rude, condescending, and considered himself better than her.

Yet, he could also be tender, gallant, and full of passion and concern. He was a dichotomy, and she couldn't regret having experienced the pleasure of getting to know the Will he kept private. The idea of losing him now devastated her, and she bent forward to press a kiss to his forehead. "Open your eyes. Wake up, Will."

He continued to thrash, so she kissed him again, her mouth gradually moving down, stopping first to kiss his nose, and then shyly touching his mouth. She'd never kissed a man before, and even in the current situation, when he was practically insensate, it still sent sparks through her. For a moment, she wanted to deepen the kiss, but it struck her as wrong to do so without him aware and consenting to being kissed.

She pulled away with a sigh and laid down beside him, knowing she could do no more for him besides offer the comfort of her presence. She couldn't bring herself to contemplate how bleak her existence would become if Fitzwilliam died, leaving her marooned alone on this island.

***

His fever broke the next morning, and he seemed far more alert than he had when she was so sure she would lose him. Lizzy remained at his side, still caring for him and refusing to leave him for more than a few minutes at a time. His appetite was still poor, but she was able to coax him to eat some of the orange fruit and a few bites of fish. His cheeks were still flushed, but she dared hope he was on the mend. "You are going to be fine, Will."

He was still weak, but he said, "I had a strange dream. You were calling for me, begging for me to come to you. It helped me find my way."

Her heart skipped a beat as she dared consider she had kept him from succumbing to the infection with her pleas the night before. "I did ask you to fight for me." Tenderly, she ran her fingers through his hair. "I am pleased you listened to me at least once, Will."

His lips twitched, though he clearly had no strength to make a stronger reaction. "Perhaps one day, you shall reciprocate and do such an amazing thing as listen to me as well, Lizzy."

Impulsively, she bent forward and kissed his cheek, though they both froze at the contact. His gaze locked with hers, and she hesitated for a moment, tempted to press her mouth to his again. Instead, she blinked and forced herself to pull back. "Let us not expect miracles, Mr. Darcy," she said before setting out. "I am going to try to catch more fish while you rest."

CHAPTER NINE

Fitzwilliam was up to moving around within a few days, feeling much better. He could admit he liked the way Lizzy fussed over him, though it was getting a little annoying at times too. When she tried to prevent him from going to fetch water that morning, he gave her a stern look. "I am perfectly capable of doing so, Lizzy. Do step aside."

With a sigh, she did so, and he plunged into the jungle. It didn't take him long to realize she was following him, and while he appreciated her concern, she was starting to feel a bit like a mother hen.

He moved ahead of her quickly, darting behind a tree as he neared the edge of the water. When she emerged a moment later, he reached out and grabbed her, pulling her against him. "You do not need to follow me, madam. I am perfectly capable of getting water."

She let out a startled screech, and he could feel her heart

pounding against her chest where his arm crossed it. She jerked away from him, turning to glare at him. "That was most uncalled for. You gave me a fright, Mr. Darcy."

His lips twitched. "I can always tell when you are quite annoyed with me, Lizzy. You call me Mr. Darcy."

She harrumphed him. "If that were true, I would be calling you Mr. Darcy all the time, Mr. Darcy." Shoulders back, she tossed her head in the air and marched away from him.

Fitzwilliam chuckled as he set about fetching water, returning to her a short time later. As he did so, he saw she was occupied in the water, clearly trying to catch more fish. He set down the bark full of water near their shelter, and as he did so, he glanced inside.

Near the leaves she used for a bed, he saw the book her father had left her. The letter was sticking out of it, and he realized abruptly the envelope was unsealed. He moved closer, keeping an eye on her as he fished it from between the book pages. The seal had been broken at some point recently, and he was certain it had been intact just days ago. His heart raced as he realized what this might mean, and though he knew it was an unforgivable intrusion, he opened the letter and quickly read it.

My Dearest Lizzy,

It is with a heavy heart that I write this, for I fear I shall not be around to see you or your sisters happily married. First, I must apologize for leaving you in such a tenuous situation. I was never very good with managing funds, so I know you will suffer for my oversight. Perhaps I should have encouraged you to marry Mr. Collins when he offered, but I could not bring myself to do so. You would have been most unhappy, and having experienced a similar marriage, I would not wish that for you.

I leave instructions for you to only open this once you are in love, and that is because I hope and pray you will find love worthy of you, one that will make you delighted, and a man who will see to your happiness every day for the rest of your lives. He should be a kind and honorable man, and he must be an intellectual match for you, my dear, or you will grow bored. It is truly a special man who will capture your heart, and I regret I will not be around to meet him. Do not give up on the idea of finding such a love. I pray you will read this letter someday, when you have a man who takes care of you and loves you as much as I have, my dearest daughter.

Love, Papa.

Darcy blinked for a moment, overcome by the raw emotion of

the letter and vowing he would be such a man. He would love Lizzy and treat her the way her father had desired. Gently, he folded the letter and returned it to the open envelope, sliding both into the book.

"What are you doing?" She sounded shrill.

He looked up, guilt most certainly visible on his face. "I was reading your letter."

She glared at him. "You had no right, Mr. Darcy. That was a private correspondence from my father."

"I know, but I suspected there was a reason you had opened it. After all, you are not to do so until you are in love." He stepped forward, his heart hammering in his chest as she dropped a fish into the sand, not noticing it. "Are you in love, Lizzy?"

She licked her lips, but she didn't answer. She didn't flee, but she didn't approach either.

Fitzwilliam stepped closer, reaching out for her and pulling her into his arms. She made no move to resist. "If you are in love, I feel I must tell you I am in love as well."

Her eyes widened. "I should not wish to hear that just because a certain gentleman feels dutybound to repeat the words, Mr. Darcy."

He laughed as he brushed his

lips against her cheek. "And I would never say such a thing if I did not mean it. I love you, Elizabeth Bennet, and I want you to be my wife. If we are stuck here, we might never be able to legally formalize our union, but the instant the option is available to us, I fully intend to make you my wife. That is, if you love me and accept?" As he spoke, he kissed her neck, making her tremble. "Do you love me, Lizzy?" He practically whispered the words against her earlobe before nibbling gently.

She trembled as she surrendered, collapsing against him. "You must know I do, Will.

When I thought I'd lost you…" She broke off, tears suddenly streaming from her eyes.

He kissed her, wanting to distract her from sadness. "I am convinced it was your voice that brought me back from the edge, Lizzy. I love you and want to be with you. I want every day of my life to be entwined with yours."

Lizzy's eyes gleamed, and she nodded as she lifted her head. He lowered his, and their lips met in a passionate kiss. He savored her taste on his lips before dipping his tongue into her mouth. She gasped at the intrusion before swaying closer, and he stroked his tongue slowly along hers, gliding carefully along the length of hers to enhance her pleasure as he tasted her. He imagined how his tongue could move in other parts of her and nearly spilled himself right then.

Before he completely lost control, he moved his mouth from hers to trail down her neck, pausing to nip the sensitive spot at the bend. She moaned and arched her neck, offering him freer access. He happily accepted, licking and sucking the spot for a long minute as she thrashed in his arms. She was so responsive to just a light touch that he couldn't wait to see her burn completely with passion.

His hands moved quickly,

grasping the hem of her nightdress and pulling it over her head. She blinked, looking dazed as she brought up an arm to cover her breasts. He intercepted it. "No. I want to see them."

She blushed but lowered her arm to her side. He looked at the pert perfection before him. "Your eyes are not the only fine part of you, Lizzy."

She giggled, though she still seemed self-conscious. That wouldn't do. He had to ensure she was swept away with passion that precluded overthinking how she felt.

He bent his head, tasting one of her nipples and almost purring with satisfaction at the way she moaned. She was delicious, and he craved more. He deepened the kiss of his mouth against her breast, sucking in her nipple as she arched her back. She seemed mad with passion, and he was pleased to see her lost in the throes of pleasure he gave her.

Carefully, he eased her onto the leaves in their shelter, kneeling between her splayed legs. Fitzwilliam kissed her other breast and explored her stomach with his mouth before inhaling the spicy scent of her arousal. She clenched and trembled when his tongue darted inside her core seconds later, and he moaned his own pleasure at her flavor and how wet she was.

He was aching to be inside her, so he brought in a hand to assist his mouth. His fingers strummed over her pearl as she twitched and bucked against him while his tongue discovered all her secrets. When she came with a cry moments later, he almost released as well. Only knowing how much better it would be inside her helped him hold back.

He moved back long enough to strip off his breeches. He hadn't bothered with the shirt this morning, so once he'd removed his boots, he was as bare as she was. He allowed her a moment to examine him with frank appraisal, realizing just how curious his Lizzy was. He fully intended to allow her full rein to explore that curiosity, but it would have to wait until the next time they made love. He needed to be inside her too badly to wait while she carefully and torturously investigated him.

She nibbled on her lip as he returned to her, cock in hand as he found her opening. "Will it hurt, Will?"

He frowned, straining to ease inside rather than thrust like an animal and rut her. "I hope it shall not, but I believe it might. I have never been with a virgin before, so I cannot say for certain."

She bit harder on her lip. "Perhaps we should do something else instead."

He managed a tight smile. "I promise you will enjoy this, even if it hurts at first."

Lizzy appeared to be mustering her courage. "Very well. I am ready, Will."

He grinned at her words, knowing she was girding herself for battle. He intended to ensure she enjoyed as much of the experience as possible.

Carefully, he surged inside her, moving slowly until he was fully seated to the hilt. She winced a couple of times, but she was blinking now. "Are you well?"

She had a hazy smile. "Very well, Will. It is most pleasurable. There was a tiny bit of pain, but it is already gone."

He heaved a sigh of relief. "In that case, do I have your permission to move?" When she nodded, he withdrew and thrust into her silken tightness again, certain he might die from the pleasure of it. He knew he wouldn't last as long as he'd like this time, so he reached between them and stroked her sensitive nub again, soon coaxing her to another climax.

Fitzwilliam spilled his seed

inside her as he lost control. She cried out her pleasure, and his shout of ecstasy mingled with hers. He was vaguely aware of the monkeys suddenly chittering excitedly in the background, but he spared no further thought for anything except Lizzy, who was his whole world.

***

They spent the next few days becoming closer, learning each other's bodies, and indulging in every passionate whim either could devise. Fitzwilliam had never been so happy, and it was for that reason alone he was tempted for the briefest moment not to light the signal fire when he saw a ship on the horizon.

Their interlude here was idyllic, with just the two of them. He couldn't imagine a more perfect existence than this, but just as quickly, he realized how selfish that would be. Lizzy deserved to have every comfort in life, and when he imagined the horror of her having to give birth with only him there when she inevitably became pregnant, he quickly rushed to their regular fire, grabbed a stick, and hurried over to the bonfire.

It was alight within minutes, and Lizzy came running from the jungle. She carried the bark they used for water in her hand, but she'd clearly abandoned any thought of getting the water. "Is there a ship?" She sounded joyous.

He nodded as he rushed toward her. "Over there." He pointed to it, his heart stuttering when he realized it was changing course to come their direction. That was what he wanted, but part of him couldn't help regretting the end of their time here on the island.

She clung to him. "Oh, this is wondrous news." Then she looked down, flinching. "I suppose it is a good thing I saved my dress." She laughed at that as she rushed over to retrieve it from her satchel in the shelter. She disappeared into the jungle, and he assumed she must fear being seen by anyone aboard the ship as she changed, since she was comfortable being nude around him now.

When she returned moments later, the wild and carefree Lizzy he'd come to know in the last few weeks was mostly gone. Her hair was still a mess, but she was dressed sedately again in the appropriate day gown, with not even her ankles revealed. He could see the very top slope of her chest, along with her bared arms, but that was it. He mourned the loss of his island Lizzy even as his heart rejoiced at the thought of returning to civilization so he could claim her properly as his bride.

It didn't seem like long at all before a longboat came to shore to rescue them. Lizzy and Fitzwilliam were both waiting to board, and the men fussed over the two of them as they rowed back to the bigger ship.

It was a welcome sight to see Charles and Miss Jane waiting for them, though he was surprised to see the two of them standing on what appeared to be a merchant ship. "I did not expect you to be along for the rescue," said Fitzwilliam to Charles as Charles clapped him on the shoulder.

"Of course, man. When we could find no further assistance

from the Navy, we approached this merchant vessel and asked them to take on a mission. We have sailed everywhere we could think of that might have followed the currents from the storm, and we found you." In his exuberance, Charles reached forward and hugged him.

Fitzwilliam could hardly reject the gesture, and he admitted it was good to have his friend nearby again as he hugged him back. Then he turned to Miss Jane, taking her hand in his and brushing his lips against her gloved knuckles. "It is lovely to see you again, Miss Bennet."

Jane giggled, and Charles

looked at her with pride. "That is Mrs. Bingley, Darcy."

He frowned as Lizzy asked, "How was such a thing accomplished so quickly?"

Jane giggled as she turned to Lizzy, hugging her for a long moment. "The captain insisted upon it."

Fitzwilliam looked at Charles with a brow cocked. "The captain?"

"He is rather a superstitious man, and he was at first dismayed at the idea of a woman being aboard at all. When I told him we were engaged—which was true— he insisted we were married before we traveled on the ship. He married us himself just last week." He hesitated, eyeing Fitzwilliam with concern. He was clearly bracing himself for his friend's opinion.

"Congratulations are in order then. She seems like a fine match for you." Though Fitzwilliam still had a few hesitations, since he didn't know Jane well enough and had only observed her through interaction with his friend, he trusted Lizzy's judgment, and she was certain Jane was in love with his friend. Charles gave every appearance of being in love with her, so how could he complain, especially since he intended to tie his future to another Bennet girl as quickly as possible?

When he looked up, Lizzy was gone, as was Jane. He looked around, catching the eye of one of the sailors. "Where has my companion gone?"

"The other miss took her belowdecks to her cabin."

Darcy nodded, but he was intercepted by the captain before he could follow. "You shall have to work to stay aboard to earn your keep until the next port, same as your friend here."

Fitzwilliam frowned. "Did Mr. Bingley not pay you good coin?"

"Aye, he did, but everyone works aboard the ship, except for the ladies. It is bad luck to have them aboard, but I suppose there is no help for it now." He turned his head and spat.

Fitzwilliam guessed he should be grateful the man hadn't spat on his boots. "What shall I do?"

"What shall you not do?" said Charles with a hint of despair.

CHAPTER TEN

Lizzy spent the next six days confined to the cabin. The captain refused to allow her to leave it, though he did let Jane move back and forth between the cabin she shared with Charles and Lizzy's to visit and bring meals. Lizzy expected Fitzwilliam to come see her, but as the days passed, it became more and more evident he wasn't going to.

Feeling out of sorts and concerned, wondering if everything he'd told her had just been words he'd said to convince her to warm his bed, she fell into despondency. When they reached America, docking in Boston on the sixth day, she still expected Darcy to seek her out, but there was no sign of him. The captain kept them aboard awhile, with Jane telling Lizzy he'd sent word ahead to have Mr. Collins meet them. When he finally told them they could get off the ship, Jane was there to accompany her, as was Charles, and they disembarked.

She was about to ask Charles where Fitzwilliam was when a portly man, who bore a strong resemblance to Mr. Collins, approached and she realized he must be Thaddeus Collins, the younger Collins brother, who had not inherited Longbourn. She knew he was a successful merchant, and she was hoping he was nothing like his older brother, except in appearance.

He greeted them with an inscrutable expression. "You must be the Bennet girls? I got word you would be arriving via this ship." He looked askance at the merchant boat. At their nod, he touched his hat. "I am most pleased to make your acquaintance, though I question your choice of vessel for the voyage." His gaze turned to Charles, and it bordered on hostile. "Who might you be, sir?"

"He is my husband," said Jane with a small giggle, still clearly delighted at being able to announce that.

Mr. Collins scowled. "Your mother did not mention you having a husband when you set out from London, Miss Bennet." He seemed most displeased, disproportionately so.

Jane didn't seem to realize, but Charles appeared to as he looked aghast. "We met aboard the ship,

Mr. Collins. Your cousin and I have been married almost two weeks."

"I shall require proof of that before I can allow you to take her into your custody, sir." Collins drew himself up, and he was quite an intimidating sight, though most of his bulk came from excess weight rather than muscles.

If Charles was intimidated, he gave no sign. "That can certainly be arranged. I have the marriage license in my luggage, but the captain can also vouch for us, since he is the one who married us." He raised his hand to gesture to the captain, who stood nearby. "Captain Darren, will you please confirm for Mr. Collins that Mrs. Bingley and I are properly wed by your hand?"

"Aye," called the captain before turning away.

Lizzy wondered for a moment if Mr. Collins would protest, but other than drawing himself up with a bit of outrage, he nodded. "Very well then. You have permission to take her." He turned his attention to Lizzy. "You will find a nice room waiting for you, and I have engaged a lady's companion as well."

Lizzy looked uncertainly at Jane and Charles, wanting to find Fitzwilliam. "I am afraid I cannot leave yet, Mr. Collins. There is someone I must speak with first."

"Nonsense. I am in a rush, and your sister has my address." He gathered her by the arm, pulling her along with him.

Lizzy didn't want to go anywhere and started to resist. "You are behaving most peculiarly, Mr. Collins."

He shook his head, looking disgruntled. "Is it no wonder? I thought I would have the choice between the two of you. I prepared myself to take on the guardianship of the other sister, for how could I not take care of my wife's family?" He smiled after a moment, though his expression revealed little true pleasure. "Of course, you are a fine choice, but Miss Jane is much more attractive, as I am certain you must concede. You no doubt hear that often."

Lizzy frowned. "I do, but I do not understand…" She trailed off as she realized suddenly that Mr. Collins had invited her and Jane here with the intention of wedding one of them and accepting the other as his burden, the price he must pay to wed one. She gasped and pulled away from him. "I shall not marry you, Mr. Collins."

He glared at her. "You most certainly shall. Not only did I pay for your passage, but I advanced your mother a hundred pounds."

Lizzy gasped, shocked at her mother's actions, though she supposed she shouldn't be. It was entirely like Fanny to send Lizzy and Jane into such a situation without warning them they were about to be married, whether they liked it or not.

When he reached for her again, she jerked away. "I cannot marry you, Mr. Collins. You see, I am already ruined." She took great pleasure in revealing she had been stranded alone on an island with Mr. Darcy for weeks.

He flinched. "Mr. Darcy? Fitzwilliam Darcy, relation to Lady Catherine de Bourgh?"

She shrugged. "I have no idea

about his relation to said lady, but it is Fitzwilliam Darcy."

He scowled, his displeasure clear. "Since he is such a fine gentleman of quality, and my brother speaks highly of Lady de Bourgh, I shall overlook the indiscretion."

Lizzy's eyes widened. "You still wish to marry me even though I was marooned alone with a man?"

He scoffed. "There will be no marriage. I shall set you up in an apartment and keep you as a mistress. It shall be a fine living for you, and it will allow me to select a more appropriate woman while still fulfilling my obligations as agreed upon with your mother."

Lizzy's jaw dropped when she tried to wrench away from him and hissed with pain when he tightened his grasp. "I highly doubt my mother agreed to me being your mistress. I will not go anywhere with you, Mr. Collins." She turned away, calling out, "Mr. Bingley, I need your help."

He and Jane had remained a few feet away, appearing undecided about how to handle Mr. Collins, but as soon as she called for him, he sprang into action. Mr. Bingley rushed toward them. When he saw Mr. Collins holding Lizzy's arm, he frowned in censure. "You will release her at once, sir."

"This is not your business, sir." Mr. Collins glared at Mr. Bingley. "I do not know who you think you are—"

"I am Charles Bingley, and that is my sister you are manhandling. You shall release her at once." As he spoke, Charles reached out and grabbed Mr. Collins, evidently undeterred by his larger size. He shoved him away and took Lizzy's hand, spiriting her away from their cousin. Lizzy expected the man to follow behind, but all he did was shout a few insults before he turned away, clearly disgruntled.

As soon as she rushed to Jane, she confessed what she had

learned. The two sisters embraced, sharing mutual horror at their mother's actions.

Mr. Bingley looked disapproving. "I shall ensure the man is reimbursed for the money he advanced your mother and the cost of your tickets, dear ladies. We have no wish for him to try to maintain any claim to either of you."

She let out a sigh of relief, though she couldn't help thinking this should be Fitzwilliam's obligation, should he actually plan to live up to his promise to marry her. She looked around again, further confused. "Where is Mr. Darcy, Mr. Bingley?"

He frowned. "No one told you?"

She shook her head. "Told me what?"

"Mr. Darcy has been rushed to the hospital. He had a healing injury on his leg from a boar, I believe he said, and he acquired another one during our forced labor for the captain. It is infected, so he is with the physicians now."

Lizzy had never been more relieved and terrified at the same time. Fitzwilliam hadn't abandoned her or his promise to her. Yet he was in mortal danger, or so it seemed, and she grasped Charles's arm. "I must get to him immediately. Will you see a hansom cab comes for me?"

He shook his head. "I shall do no such thing. I have a driver waiting already, and Jane and I will accompany you to the hospital."

She smiled in gratitude, soon finding herself in the cab beside her sister. Jane reached out to hold her hand, offering silent comfort, as Lizzy tortured herself imagining how ill Fitzwilliam must be if he had not been able to see her off the ship, or to see her at all in the last six days.

CHAPTER ELEVEN

He was more alert than she had expected, though he was still burning with fever. The doctor she consulted with told her he was likely to make a full recovery, but he needed rest first. Lizzy took the seat beside his bed, holding his hands. "This is a familiar sight," she teased gently.

"Will you kiss me again now

that I am feverish?" Even though he was clearly unwell, he still managed a playful tone.

Her eyes widened. "I did not think you remembered that." She flushed, though it was silly to be embarrassed after the intimacies they had shared during the last week of their stay at the island. "You never mentioned it."

He shrugged. "I feared it would embarrass you to do so, and I had no need to remind you when you fell right into my plans." He winked at her.

"You had plans for me, Mr. Darcy?" She fluttered her eyelashes, even as she flinched at the heat in his skin when she brushed her hand against his brow.

"Most nefarious ones. As soon as I realized being stranded on the island afforded me the perfect reason to make you my wife, a reason no one could object to, even my fearsome aunt, I fully intended to take advantage of it." He lowered his voice. "I had wanted you from practically the moment I met you, Lizzy. Part of the reason I reacted so harshly to you was because I knew the match was not a suitable one. The more time I spent with you, the less I cared, until it did not matter at all. Now, will you live up to your promise to be my wife?"

Lizzy didn't hesitate. "I shall marry you the very second we are able to. I would even accept the captain marrying us as he did for Jane and Charles."

He grimaced. "If I never see Captain Darren again, I shall be too happy. He worked Charles and I like slaves. The threat of being tossed overboard kept us from protesting, especially when trying to protect you and Miss Jane. I did not have even a moment to slip away to see you."

She gasped, relief filling her again. "Oh, thank goodness."

He frowned. "You did not wish to see me?"

She patted his chest. "Do not be

offended, dearest. I am simply relieved you had a reason not to visit me for the six days we were trapped on that ship. The captain was a superstitious man, and he would not allow me to leave my cabin and move around. He said having any woman aboard was bad luck, but particularly an unmarried one. I could not come to see you, and you did not come see me, so I started to think certain things." She blinked rapidly, looking down. "Dark thoughts I do not wish to revisit."

His expression was full of tender concern. "They were nothing more than horrible flights of imagination. I have every intention of marrying you, and we shall reside happily, whether it is here in America or back in London."

Quickly, Lizzy shared Mr. Collins's plans for her and Jane, and she found herself laughing toward the end. "He was a most horrible fellow, and I think he gives me a new appreciation for the elder Mr. Collins. His brother can be a loquacious fool, and he has his moments of smugness and insults as well, but he is nothing like his younger brother." She shuddered. "I cannot imagine where we would be if my mother and I and my sisters had been at his mercy instead of Mr.

Collins's."

"None of you shall be at any of the Collinses's mercy from now on. Once our affairs are settled, and everything is in order, I shall ensure your mother and sisters receive a generous allowance and a house suitable for them. They will no longer be reliant on the munificence of Mr. Collins."

She couldn't resist the urge to lean forward and kiss him. She meant to kiss his cheek, but he turned his mouth at the last minute and engaged her in a passionate exchange instead. Regretfully, she pulled away, though she didn't want to. "I suspect you are not in any shape for this yet, Fitzwilliam."

He frowned. "I do not know how to take that."

She cocked her brow. "Pardon?"

"When I am in your favor, I am Will. When I have displeased you, I am Mr. Darcy. So, I do not know how to interpret Fitzwilliam. Are you pleased with me, but not as pleased as you could be? Or are you displeased, but not as displeased as you have been in the past?" His eyes gleamed, and though it could've been from fever, it appeared to be from wicked delight in his banter instead.

She frowned at him. "You should be resting rather than

engaging me like this, Will. Fitzwilliam means I am content with you, and it is expected I shall call you Fitzwilliam when we are in public, is it not?" At his nod, she leaned closer, brushing her lips against his ear when she said, "However, you will always be my Will, and I will be your Lizzy whenever we are alone. I look forward to our wedding night and being island Lizzy and Will once more."

He seemed to be breathing a little harder when she pulled back, and he brought the hand she was holding to his mouth to kiss her fingers through the glove. "I am most eager for that moment as well, Elizabeth."

His eyes gleamed, and she was unable to resist kissing him once more, though they were soon interrupted by a sister who bustled in and scolded them, clearly shocked by their behavior. If Darcy was bothered by her chastisements, he gave no indication. Instead, he said, "She is already my wife in every way that matters, Sister, and the legalities will soon be dealt with. Do leave us alone."

With a huff of outrage, the sister bustled out of the room while Lizzy smothered a laugh. "How shameful of you, Will."

He seemed not at all repentant.

"I shall not allow anything to come between us, my dear love, including a sister with a starched wimple and even starchier mindset."

She giggled as she laid down on the bed beside him, uncaring about the lectures they would receive when staff saw her curled up with him so scandalously. It was worth it to be this close to Will, who would soon be her husband, and their future together would be secure.

EPILOGUE

Four months later, Lizzy was relieved to return to England and set foot on the docks in London, though not nearly as relieved as Will seemed to. He was still a little green, continuing to fight seasickness, which had gotten worse the closer they got to shore as the waves increased. She was experiencing a touch of that herself, but hers was because of her pregnancy. Otherwise, she'd never had trouble sailing.

Jane looked a little peaked as well, and Lizzy suspected it was because she was in a similar state. Her sister's pregnancy was obvious, where Lizzy's was not yet, but they were both well pleased their children would be born close to each other. She dared hope they would grow up as close as siblings.

"It is good to be back," said Charles.

"Most assuredly," said Fitzwilliam. He'd made no secret of how much he disliked America.

Lizzy had tried to be more

openminded, but she had found it equally unappealing. There were some genuinely nice people in Boston society, but it was a completely different environment than she was used to, and she was far more comfortable in the wilds around Longbourn than she was in the cramped spaces of Boston, or in London, for that matter.

She and Fitzwilliam would stay at Darcy House for a few days before they went on to Longbourn to retrieve her mother and sisters. After that, they would depart for Pemberley.

The house Darcy had commissioned to be built on Pemberley land for her mother and sisters should be finished by now, and she was looking forward to sharing the surprise with her family, though she intended to exchange a few sharp words with her mother about how she had almost maneuvered Lizzy and Jane into one of them being forced to marry the undesirable younger Mr. Collins.

Darcy put a hand on her stomach as they started walking down the wharf, the smell of fish making her queasy. "We shall soon move past the smells."

She nodded. "How is your stomach, Mr. Darcy?"

"Now it is filled with nerves that you are calling me Mr. Darcy.

What have I done to displease you?"

Lizzy laughed. "I am simply teasing, Will. Are you well though?"

He nodded. "I am quite well, and as soon as we are settled at the townhouse, and assuming you are up for it, I am most intent on showing you just how robust I am."

Lizzy smiled, looking forward to that. "I like the way you think, Will. I am certain I will be quite well by then too." He held her hand in his as they walked along, soon meeting with their carriage.

Charles and Jane departed from them, intent on reaching the

Bingley townhouse, and she'd see her sister soon enough, since Jane planned to travel with them to Longbourn and then on to Pemberley for a while. Jane was hoping Charles would buy property near Pemberley, and Lizzy hoped for the same. Though they were both married women, they would continue to be close and in each other's lives on a frequent basis.

For now, she was content to have Fitzwilliam to herself. She hoped she could coax out the wild Will she remembered from the island, and she doubted she would have any difficulty doing so.

In private, they were still Lizzy

and Will, and they had not lost the free-spiritedness they had found on the island, nor their deep love for each other. It only continued to grow, and she was confident it would always be that way.

***

ABOUT THE AUTHOR

Abbey is a diehard Jane Austen fan and has loved Fitzwilliam since the first time she "met" him at age thirteen upon borrowing the book from the school library. He is the ideal man, though Abbey's husband is a close second. Abbey enjoys writing various steamy and sweet Jane Austen variations, but "Pride & Prejudice" (and Mr. Darcy) will always be her favorite.